Dedicated to our families—
our children, parents, grandparents, all who are no longer with us,
and to those who are yet to be born.
E.LZ. & J.T.

First Edition 2012

Second Printing 2013
China

Book design by Eileen L. Ziesler and Janelle Thompson
The text of this book is set in Papyrus. The illustrations are water color reproduced in full color.

Summary: When a new life is born into a family it is good to remember the ancestors,
the gifts they have given and the communities in which they lived.

Library of Congress Control Number: 2011945362

Ziesler, Eileen L.
    Little Sprout : a poem / by Eileen L. Ziesler ; illustrated by Janelle Thompson. -- 1st ed.

    Interest age level: 003-007.
    ISBN: 978-0-9818831-5-1

e-ISBN: 978-0-9818831-6-8

Toad House Publishing

Little Sprout

The story of your family tree

Poem by Eileen L. Ziesler
Illustrated by Janelle L. Thompson

Here you are,
a little sprout.

JANELLE THOMPSON

You are so loved, there is no doubt.

JANELLE THOMPSON

You will grow
and grow
and grow.

We are the trees and we know.

JANELLE THOMPSON

Your mom and dad were once like you,

JANELLE THOMPSON

Little sprouts who grew and grew,

Janelle Thompson

Sheltered from the wind and storm

By moms and dads who kept them warm.

JANELLE THOMPSON

Your grandparents,
they were once like you,

Just little sprouts who grew and grew,

With their parents who
loved them too.

JANELLE THOMPSON

Yes! Your grandparents grew and grew.

Great grandparents? Of course like you!

Once were sprouts who grew and grew.

From the leaves and branches tall

JANEIIE THOMPSON

Of trees around when they were small.

JANELLE THOMPSON

In this woods
the old trees rest

And still give you the very best.

From your roots
you too will grow,

From these trees so long ago.

JANELLE THOMPSON

We all love you,
Little Sprout,

JANELLE THOMPSON

And with this love you'll grow, no doubt.

JANELLE THOMPSON

You will grow
and grow
and grow.

JANELLE THOMPSON

We are the trees, and we know.

Who do you s

This is a place to remember all the people who love yo

your family tree?

Write in their names and glue in their pictures.

A note from the author:

When my son called with the joyful news of the birth of his son in early autumn, I became a grandmother for the first time. It was also the season that my father began to take his leave. The power of new life and imminent death collided that night, and I awoke at 3:00 in the morning to hear myself reciting the words of Little Sprout.

Two months later in the intensive care unit, my daughter-in-law held up her son so his great-grandfather could see him for the first and last time. My father came briefly out of his coma to meet this new life, his great-grandson. He saw and understood that our family tree had new growth. He smiled and gestured to the little one who gazed back at him.

After my father's death, I visited the poem many times, especially the lines, "In this woods the old trees rest and still give you the very best. From your roots you too will grow, from these trees so long ago."

I look at my grandchildren and other young children in my community. I wonder what they will take from the cradle knoll of their ancestry.

What our children learn from the family stories they hear will help shape how they view their place in this world. If they are so blessed, they will experience the same emotions of love, new life, and death as those who came before; because we are all trees in the forest of Little Sprout.

A note from the artist:

When given this children's poem to illustrate, I wondered what visual theme I should use to depict the story. It soon became clear that the metaphor of the little sprout in the forest had many parallels in human life.

We can examine how even the negative events in our lives; like a fire or a storm in the life of a forest, can bring about positive change and new birth. Seeds may break open in the heat of the fire to become new trees. An old tree, dying from decay, may become a cradle knoll with nutrients for many species of bugs and fungus, which in turn shelter and feed other species.

As you read through the book, notice the supporting cast on the left side of the page. You might think of the animals and plants on the left page like friends and extended family, all playing a role in the life of the little sprout.

Notice what is happening to the forest on the right-hand pages as you read through the book. The forest is aging in reverse. The cradle knoll on one page will be the fallen log later in the story. This fallen log will become an old tree and going back further, the tree will be young—a little sprout.

I hope you enjoy seeing these forest relationships; and that they lead you to talk to your child about the ecology of the forest, your own family ancestry, and your child's place in your family and in the world. We invite you to place your family names and photos in this book.

A Lullaby for Little Sprout

Eileen L. Ziesler
Copyright 2011